Shadows of the Mind

Edited by H. C. Kilgour

Shadows of the Mind

Edited by H. C. Kilgour

To everyone.
We all have our days.
Let the good outweigh the bad.

Table of Contents

Men: The Unsaid

by Anisha Singh

Aditya is a brilliant high school student. His charisma and infectious smile light up any room. Although English is not his first language, he speaks it well. His deep, soothing voice captivates every girl. But when he comes home, his parents' high expectations weigh on him like an anchor.

One evening, Aditya stepped out to buy groceries. His mind raced with thoughts about school and expectations. Distracted, he misstepped and fell hard onto the pavement, scraping his knee. He hissed in pain as a tear slid down his cheek.

A passerby looked down at him and with disdain, saying, "Man up; it's just a scrape."

The comment stung. It reminded Aditya how society often trivializes men's pain, both physical and emotional. *Why do we acknowledge the pain of a scraped knee with ease but overlook men's deeper struggles? Why don't we acknowledge that men can even have these struggles?* he thought. In a world that glorifies stoicism, Aditya felt the weight of the expectations from society and those closer to home. He questioned whether he could ever escape these norms and express his true feelings without being told to feel ashamed.

He wasn't allowed to play cricket in the evening; his parents believed leisure time was a waste. Cricket wouldn't provide him a good future; a good education would do that. Every day his friends invited him to join their cricket games and he had to decline. The laughter of his peers always felt like a distant echo, mocking him from afar. Their constant pressure and taunts made him feel more alone. He often wonders if he'll ever be free to do what he wants.

That night, standing on the balcony and looking down, Aditya felt overwhelmed. He thought, *Should I jump and end it all? Won't it be better to be free than to keep studying and feeling so lonely? What's the point of life if I'm not living it for me?*

His phone rang, breaking the negative thoughts' hold. It was a call from one of his classmates. Aditya hesitated for a moment but decided to go inside and answer it. Talking with his friend helped. It calmed his worries, and he slept well that night.

ΔΔΔ

The next morning, as birds chirped and people bustled outside, Aditya got ready for school. He felt a mix of anticipation and dread—why he couldn't say. As he came downstairs, he saw a moving truck parked across the street.

"Someone must have moved into the neighborhood," he said to himself.

He saw a girl in a red floral dress, her flowing hair shining in the sunlight. Her face was lit up, making her look like a radiant angel. His heart fluttered at the sight.

His mother called out to him, pulling him back to reality. When he went to look for the girl again, she was gone. On his way to school, he couldn't stop thinking about her. Who was she? How could he get to know her?

After school, he asked his mother, "Maa, has anyone moved into our block?"

She replied, "Yes, a newlywed couple and the sister of the husband."

"Bit odd for the sister to move with them," Aditya commented.

"Their parents live in the countryside," Maa explained. "The local school is small, and they wanted their daughter to have a good education. I believe she'll be starting at your school soon."

Aditya couldn't stop a smile from shaping his lips. He looked outside his window, hoping for another glimpse of her, but saw nothing but the buys street. As night fell and darkness enveloped him, he tossed and turned in his bed, unable to sleep. Unable to stop imagining all the ways their first introduction could go.

The next morning felt different. As usual, he got ready for school, but this time with excitement bubbling inside him. It would be the girl's first day.

The usual morning assembly prayer took place and then it was time for first class. Right away, his teacher was introducing everyone to Reya.

Their teacher advised Reya, "You can get help from Aditya and Kritika. They are the best students in the class."

When Reya looked at Aditya, time seemed to stand still. He was awestruck.

In a rare burst of confidence—or desperation—he shouted, "Yes, sir!"

The other students stared, laughing, wondering what had gotten into him.

During lunch break, Aditya mustered up his courage

and approached Reya. "Hey."

"Hi," replied Reya with a warm smile.

"I know you're new here, so feel free to ask for anything if you need help," Aditya offered.

"Thank you," Reya said.

He couldn't explain it, but Reya felt like a ray of hope and in that moment, Aditya felt true happiness. It was a brief escape from his heavy, negative emotions.

ΔΔΔ

The next day, Reya asked Aditya for his English notes. He was happy to oblige and took it as a chance to connect. After school, they stayed on campus and Aditya helped her with the earlier chapters.

"Do you watch the Shaktimaan show?" asked Aditya as their study session was drawing to a close.

"No," Reya replied, her cheeks flushing as if embarrassed.

"Come to my house. We can watch it after school on Saturday," Aditya suggested. He was really hoping for a yes.

Reya hesitated, glancing at the floor. Then shook her head, saying, "No, I have to study since I joined in the middle of the session." She then left in a hurry.

Aditya could only stare at her retreating figure; already he knew he was falling in love. Not going out to play cricket stopped bothering him and thoughts of Reya completely consumed him and he felt a little less lonely. He visited temple to thank Lord Krishna for sending Reya into his life. Now, going to school was the highlight of his day, and seeing her face brought him unparalleled joy.

Over the next two months, his life became exciting.

He began to participate in all the activities that Reya participated in. Aditya joined debates, quizzes, basketball games, and cultural dances to spend more time with Reya. Their connection grew stronger with each day and activity. It was a love story in the making.

ΔΔΔ

And Aditya's affection was not one-sided. Reya had felt anxious about moving to the city—it was her first time living in an urban area. She'd worried she wouldn't fit in and would continue to be alone. Her village was small and though there were a few girls her age, they had never really been friends.

As the days passed, Reya grew more grateful for Aditya's presence. Her anxiety about moving to the city changed to a sense of belonging; his unwavering support and encouragement made it happen. She often reflected on how much she had changed since arriving. The bustling city, once daunting, now felt vibrant and full of possibilities. With each moment, her feelings for Aditya deepened. He was more than a friend; he understood her.

She realized she had started liking Aditya because she wouldn't write for just anyone. Reya's favorite thing was to write and poetry—especially writing poetry— was her love language. Living in the countryside with few people to talk to had made her use writing as her primary form of expression. Writing for someone felt like sharing herself.

On Aditya's birthday, Reya surprised him with a poem she had written—a heartfelt expression of her feelings. She believed writing was a better way to express her emotions than speaking.

A boy full of faith, filled with kindness,
A beautiful soul, a blessing to the world.
A fantastic friend with a heart so pure,
In your presence, joy and love unfurl.

Your energy spreads like a pleasant breeze.
Refreshing the surroundings and brightening the room.
A mentor who empowers others—helping them shine,
Opening doors to opportunities and making dreams align.

Your immense belief in others is a ray of light.
Guiding us through the darkest hours of the night.
Through life's ebb and flow, you stand strong,
Inspiring us all to keep moving along.

For the love that you share and the dreams you pursue,
May your journey ahead be filled with few failures and countless triumphs.
May you keep shining bright in the vastness of the universe.

Happy birthday, Aditya

When she presented him with the handwritten poem on his birthday, she could tell Aditya was captivated by it.

"This is incredibly thoughtful," he said, his eyes sparkling. "You have a real talent for words. Thank you; it means a lot."

Reya's cheeks flushed with warmth, and she lit up with a radiant smile.

ΔΔΔ

Aditya, still feeling the warmth of Reya's poem, grinned as he handed her two chocolates. "Here's a sweet treat for a sweet person. You made my birthday special."

Reya accepted the chocolates. "Thank you."

After sharing a warm smile, they both said goodbye to their friends before heading home together. It was extremely convenient for their growing feelings that they lived on the same street.

Aditya felt flattered—on cloud nine—no one had ever written anything for him before.

When Aditya arrived home from school, there was an unsettling silence that filled the house. He approached his parents' room with caution and overheard their conversation.

"It's been hard lately, business is slow, and we have bill to pay," he heard his father say. "We may need to move into a house with cheaper rent or to a less expensive area. I'm sorry I couldn't make it work."

"Honey," his mother starts, "when we got married, we vowed to be together through every phase of our lives. I know you tried your best. Whatever you decide, we are in this together."

His father spoke in a low voice, "I must have done something good in a previous life to deserve marrying you."

Aditya's world crumbled. His parents' words sliced through his dreams like a cold wind. Panic surged within him. He wanted to scream, to beg them not to leave. Instead, he stood frozen in silence as despair enveloped him like a heavy fog. He retreated to his room and loneliness crept in, a chilling contrast to his warm, cherished memories.

Aditya, his eyes red and glazed with exhaustion, walked into school the next day and sought out Reya beneath their favorite tree. He took a deep breath, struggling to find the right words. "I want to…" he began, but his voice fumbled, dissolving into hesitation.

"What is it?" Reya prompted, her brow furrowing with concern.

Overwhelmed by emotion, tears spilled down Aditya's cheeks. "I want to be here with you," he sobbed.

Reya's face shifted from surprise to compassion, and she wrapped her arms around him. "I'm here—I'm listening," she murmured.

Looking into her eyes, which sparkled with empathy, Aditya felt a ray of hope. "Before you came into my life, I was miserable. You brought color and joy back into my world. And now that I've learned to embrace life again, it feels like I might lose everything." His words hung in the air, heavy with unspoken fears and dreams.

They both grappled with the uncertainty that lay ahead.

"I like you too," Reya confessed, her voice soft but filled with sincerity. "You've given me hope as well." Her eyes sparkled with unshed tears, reflecting the warmth of the moment.

Aditya smiled, a sense of determination washing over him. "I will email you. I'll write. We'll find a way to stay in touch," he promised, his voice steady and reassuring.

"Know that I will always be there for you," Reya replied. Her gaze drifted to the horizon where the sun was setting. "Whenever you miss me, watch the sunsets or gaze at the moon—I'll be watching too."

The idea of their bond, despite the distance, brought Aditya bittersweet comfort. They stood in silence, the air charged with an unspoken understanding. It was as if time had paused, allowing them to savor this fragile moment while the sunset's vibrant colors painted the sky orange and pink. In that stillness, they both knew no matter the challenges ahead, they would carry each other's hopes and dreams.

Later that evening, as Aditya sat at the dinner table, an uneasy silence filled the air.

His mother's voice broke the tension as she said, "We need to move, Aditya. Dad's business is deeply in debt, and we're struggling to make ends meet. You'll have to change schools, too."

Aditya's heart raced, all the pent-up emotions surging within him like a volcano ready to erupt. Then, he did explode. "And what if I don't want to move? Have you ever considered what I want? You have no idea how I've felt!" His voice echoed off the walls, filled with frustration. "You never let me play cricket or do anything I want! Sometimes I feel like a robot just following your instructions. Why do I have to be caged? Why don't you let me do things my way?" He left the table abruptly.

A few hours later, Aditya's dad quietly entered his room. Aditya was sitting on the edge of the bed, lost in thought.

His father looked at him and said, "When I was your age, we had only one school nearby, and we had to walk a kilometer to get there. We didn't have many resources. That's why we want you to focus on your studies—to get good grades and live a stable life. We never wanted you to suffer."

Aditya turned to look at him.

"Times have changed," he continued. "At your new school, you can play cricket and make new friends. And every Sunday, I'll even play cricket with you."

Aditya was moved by the gesture. It took a lot to admit that good intentions had gone awry. He hugged his dad tightly. "I'm sorry."

His father returned the embrace. "It's okay, son. We're all learning. But if anything is bothering you, please come to me. I'm here for you."

Aditya's mom comes to stand in the doorway. "How about we go out for ice cream?"

Aditya walked over to her, wrapping his arms around her in a firm embrace. "I'm sorry, Maa. I behaved in a manner that wasn't suitable."

She smiled, "It's okay, beta. You are our sunshine, our happiness. Let's go enjoy some ice cream."

And out for ice cream they went. It was a simple gesture, but it symbolized love, care, and support. In the end, everything got sorted out. A cold treat warmed their hearts amidst shared laughter. That night, Aditya felt relieved.

On his last day at his old school, Aditya met with all his teachers. He thanked them for their guidance. As he was about to leave, surrounded by friends, everyone took turns writing heartfelt messages on his T-shirt. It was a memorable way to say goodbye.

When he turned to Reya, she smiled with tears in her eyes. She seemed to be frozen for a moment as she held back her emotions. She promised, "I will keep writing poems for you."

Aditya wanted to wrap Reya in his arms, but with everyone around he held her hands instead. "You are irreplaceable in my heart. We will stay in touch; take care of yourself."

As they parted ways, Aditya felt hopeful that their paths would cross again someday. Walking home, a wave of nostalgia washed over him. He realized that this place would forever hold a special place in his heart.

A Letter to Men
by Anisha Singh

Dear Men,

Hello! How are you doing?

We want to remind you that your worth extends far beyond your profession. You are more than your job. You are beautiful, inside and out. Your dreams shine in your eyes. Your passion and playfulness make life worth living. Your vulnerability is strength, not weakness.

Don't be afraid to show emotions and express your fears and doubts. We are here to listen without judgment. You are so much more than societal expectations. Embrace your true selves. We love and value you. You are our rock on stormy nights and our warmth in winter's chill. You complete our lives. Your presence brings vibrancy to our lives. Without you, everything feels dull and pale.

Know that you are never alone; we stand beside you through life's joys and challenges. Don't suffer alone; don't suppress your emotions. The more you express, the more we can support and help you navigate life's challenges.

Sincerely,
Women

The Speech

Joyce Bou Charaa

I'm so happy I'm leaving this place tomorrow. Forever. Those boring classes where I used to sit all alone looking out the window. At lunch breaks I used to glance at the empty chairs when all my classmates were out in the sunshine, enjoying the weather and each other's company; I had no one to sit with or talk to. Just me, myself, and I.

But I'm leaving my solitude now, my killing loneliness, and I'm going somewhere better—to find real friends, to sit with them all day long, to create happy memories. I will move on and change myself. That's right, I will stop being a shy girl who's afraid of talking to other people. From now on there's going to be a new me, and everyone will love her. I just don't want people to laugh at me anymore; I want people to laugh with me, so we can laugh together. I want lots of things, and I'm going to make them <u>*happen*</u>*. The old me doesn't exist anymore; she's buried forever, lost and never to be found.*

Catherine stopped writing her diary as her mother came into her room. She doesn't want to show her what's really on the inside.

"Cathy," her mother said brightly, "I just brought

your dress from the tailor. She did an incredible job. Can't wait to see you wearing it tomorrow night."

"Yeah, whatever," Catherine huffed.

"Why aren't you excited? When I was your age, I couldn't sleep the night before graduation. I was the happiest person in the world."

Catherine didn't reply, instead staring at her diary in her lap. She was happy about graduation, albeit for a very different reason than her mother.

"Oh, I see! You're preparing your speech."

"Uh, yes. It's a bit long, so I need to be ready. Need to have it memorized," Catherine mumbled.

"Alright, dear. Well, when you finish, I'll show you a short dress of mine that you're going to love."

"A dress for what?"

"For the after-party."

"Mom… I'm not going to the afterparty." Catherin still didn't know how her mother had never noticed her unpopularity.

Why not? All your friends will be there; you'll have so much fun. Also, you'll get the chance to talk with the guy you told me you like—"

"I'm not going!" Catherine snapped. "Just leave me alone, okay."

Catherine hadn't told her about her not having any friends at school, nor that some of her classmates made fun of… bullied her short stature. She was hiding this from her parents; they wouldn't have understood, just saying there were much worse things than being short. And as for the guy that she likes, Catherine has kept her feelings to herself. He was the only person in school that didn't make fun of her; he seemed to respect her and talked with her from time to time. But he was popular, suave and charismatic; how could she admit to him she liked him?

Right now, Catherine just wanted to focus on finishing her speech letter for the graduation ceremony tomorrow night. Then high school would be over. Finally.

"I'm going to make it. I'm going to be so strong and confident in front of everyone tomorrow," she kept saying to herself.

Then graduation came, and Catherine was doing her best to look happy in front of her parents. She went with her mother to get her hair and makeup done. After she finished, she put on the final touches from the dress to the high heels to the accessories. And there was just enough time to review her speech one last time. Catherine was going to prove herself in front of her classmates. She was going to show them she could be outgoing. To help steady herself, she repeated the speech mentally on the way to the auditorium.

The ceremony began at 7 pm. Her classmates were stepping into line to walk to their seats before the main stage. As valedictorian, Catherine was the first in line.

It was a special day for the entire school, but especially coordinators and teachers. It was their time to be proud of their students who were now stepping into a new chapter of their educational lives. It was their time to be proud of the way they had shaped these young minds and prepared them to become a part of society.

Catherine and her classmates were given their cue and they paraded to their seats before the stage. Though her back was to the gathered mass of friends and family, she could still sense the pride and joy radiating from everyone.

The principal opened the graduation ceremony with a quick welcome speech. Then an administrator and two well-loved teachers gave their own speeches on the values of education and what futures awaited the graduating students.

Then, it was Catherine's turn. But before she went up on stage, Mrs. Anderson began introducing Catherine, speaking highly of her accomplishments. Even before she stood, Catherine could feel all eyes on her. With a deep breath, she stood, looking for her speech that she'd left on the empty seat next to her, but it was gone.

"Lost your speech, Catherine?" said Emily with a little laugh from the row behind her.

Catherine knew immediately that Emily had stolen the speech. This wasn't something new, but of all the times for Emily to pull something like this, this was the worst. Emily liked to hide Catherine's stuff from her and make fun of her for being "absentminded". No one ever believed that Emily had taken her things. Emily was Catherine's greatest fear. She was a truly terrible person, thriving off tormenting students from other grades with her clique. Everyone who wasn't popular avoided her. Even some of her classmates that were popular avoided her.

Oh, God! Why is this happening to me? I think I'm gonna throw up. Catherine was totally panicked.

"Please give Catherine a round of applause," Mrs. Anderson said, motioning to the podium.

Which was Catherine's cue to come up on stage.

After a polite round of clapping, silence hung over the crowd like a banket. Catherine had no choice but go up on stage—ready or not. She felt like she was about to cry, tears welling in her eyes as she looked at the audience, not knowing what to say, desperately trying to remember some words or sentences from her speech.

It wasn't until she saw her parents smiling at her that she closed her eyes, took a deep breath, and started to speak.

"Good evening, I… I just want to say that… um, today is a remarkable day for all of us. We're about to start a new adventure, a new life with so many new people. It's going to be a fresh chapter. True, we'll be leaving everything behind—good memories, maybe some bad ones. But we'll be making new memories too. I would like to thank all our teachers who gave us the best they could; their efforts to help us understand what we want to become in the future. So, thank you all, for everything."

The crowd applauded for the teachers, who were sitting on the stage. A few gave waves while others just smiled.

She was still trying to remember what her speech was about and was doing her best to appear confident.

"Then, um… I would like to thank my parents. I would like to promise them and promise myself to be the best I can going forward. The Catherine that is standing here before you all will not be the same—she will never be the same again. She will start a new path and find new people who truly love her, respect her, and appreciate her uniqueness. I'm going to be better than before, and much stronger. We all will.

"So, to everyone attending: my teachers, my parents, and my classmates, I will make you all proud of me one day. We will all make all of those that matter to us proud.

"Finally, um… I would like to thank Mr. Hamilton, our principal, for his efforts and dedication to turning our school into one of the best in Boston. So, on behalf of my class, thank you so much. Thank you all, have a wonderful evening. And don't celebrate too hard!"

After Catherine's speech, all attendees gave an enthusiastic applause. Everyone except for Emily stood. A few whistles even came from her classmates! While Catherine's eyes were full of tears, they were happy tears now and she was incredibly grateful for what just happened. That moment had passed in the best way possible. She had just proven to herself she could be confident even before daunting circumstances.

Soon Catherine and her classmates were throwing their hats into the air amongst vibrant cheers. Everyone filed from the auditorium, presumably to take pictures with their families and being the celebration in earnest.

Mrs. Anderson approached Catherine. "Catherine, that speech you just gave wasn't the one you'd been preparing if I recall correctly. What happened?"

"Mrs. Anderson, I'm so sorry, I lost it. I wasn't sure what else to do."

"I believe I saw it in Emily's hands. When I asked her about it, she told me everything."

"Well, I—"

"Catherine, you don't have to be afraid of her. Or anyone. You should have the courage to tell the truth. Emily is a young girl like you, she's so confident and brave, and I know very well she bullied a lot of students, including you. But no one ever said anything to me because you were all afraid of her. And teachers can't usually do a whole lot unless someone speaks up."

"Mrs. Anderson, I… from now on, I promise you I will do my best to be a strong, confident girl."

"Don't promise me that. Promise yourself that. You know you're my favorite student, and I always want the best for you. So, promise yourself first to be that girl, and work on it for your own self. Congratulations, dear."

Catherine gave her teacher a hug full of respect and love. Mrs. Anderson had always been a big support for Catherine, and now she shared with her the most important lesson Catherine had ever learned.

Breathe In, Breathe Out

by Diya Lekshmi P. N.

Breathe in. Breathe out.

The water stands right at my ribs, its cold hands gripping my skin, digging its nails in, trying to restrain me. There is a certain comfort to the water needling my skin.

Breathe in. Breathe out.

I close my eyes, feeling the winter air brush past me, nudging me to move ahead. There is no reason to hold back, but I have been staid. I need a few more minutes. I just need time.

Breathe in. Breathe out.

I needed to sit down. Sitting down would help. It would hurt for a while I knew. First, the water would grab me by the legs, pulling me in before strangling me, gripping as hard as it could while I tried to fight its claws.

Why would I fight? Why *should* I fight? I should have taken the pills. I can't turn back now. I should live through at least the last few seconds I have, shouldn't I? Or should I have opted for comfort? Comfort would have been great. No cold water. Not much to run away from. I shake off my thoughts, focusing on the water around me.

What would happen after I give in?

My chest would start to burn, and I would try to swim up. It would be of no help. The water would be too strong. I wouldn't be able to see the sky again. The fight would be halfway over by then, all my chances dissolved with whatever regrets I might have.

Breathe in. Breathe out.

The water would slither into my mouth while I would be dragged away from shore. The desperate embrace of the water would subside for the water would have already accepted my decision. How could it save a man who didn't want to save himself?

Breathe in. Breathe out.

The sand shifted beneath my feet again, an invisible pull urging me deeper, closer to the edge where the water would tower over me. My toes dig into the cold, damp grains, anchoring me. I feel myself being pressed down, like the sky has decided to rest on my shoulders. It's hard to breathe.

"Breathe in. Breathe out," I murmured to myself, lips quivering as I open my eyes again.

The world is a muted grey, the horizon blending into the dull water, like they were meant to swallow each other. The wind hasn't stopped nudging me forward; it wants me to step in, wants me to sink. The temptation clings to me, wrapping around my chest, scratching at my ribs, trying to pluck out my heart.

Sit down. The words echo in my head. It ss a simple set of instruction. *Sit down.* I glance at my feet. *Sit down.* But my legs… they won't move.

Why am I still here?

My fingers twitch at my sides. The cold water nips at them, not yet biting, not yet dragging me under. I can feel it waiting, its patience wearing thin. I think about how easy it would be. One small step. I don't even need to sit. My body would vanish, flowing along with the water somewhere far and my footprints would no longer remain on the sand.

Breathe in. Breathe out.

The sky overhead started to shift, a crack of light breaking through the clouds. I blink, my chest still feeling tight. My voice presses against my throat while tears pool in my eyes, threatening to fall. I know what the water wants from me, and I want the same. Yet, I stay, shivering in the salty water.

I close my eyes again. If I just stepped in, all of this would end. The heaviness, the suffocating noise in my head, the endless swirling thoughts. But standing here feels worse. Tears run down my cheeks and into the water.

Breathe in. Breathe out.

I am waiting for something—a signal? I don't know. *Why can't I give in?*

Maybe it is the wind, still teasing me forward, or maybe it is the light breaking through the gray sky above. I don't want to feel cold anymore. I don't want to go with the water.

Time. I needed time.

Breathe in. Breathe out.

My hands clench into fists. My legs are still frozen in place, but I can feel the pull of the sand starting to ease. My body isn't leaning forward anymore, and the water isn't so close to my nose. I take a step back.

One step.

The water loosens its grip, its cold fingers no longer piercing me.

Another step.

My feet slip slightly in the sand, but I don't stop. I'm not sure why. The water doesn't seem as strong anymore and my mind doesn't seem as loud. The voices have hushed themselves.

I needed to run.

Breathe in. Breathe out.

The cold air embraces me again like a velvet blanket. It doesn't hurt anymore. I gaze at the sky; the gray clouds are shifting and a lighter blue hue has set in.

Breathe out. Breathe out. Breathe out.

My feet find firmer ground, the water now only hugging my ankles. I look back for a moment. Did it always look so pretty?

I turn away. The waves are still there, but they no longer feel like claws. It is just… water. No longer here to save me or drown me, just reluctantly lapping at my ankles.

Breathe in. Breathe out.

I take one more step further away.

Then another.

I can go somewhere new. Start something new. I can try again and again. Right?

A few more steps back, and I am running. Am I running away? I don't know. I am simply running.

The air is cold, and the sun is peeking out from behind the clouds, warm rays striking the ground. My teeth no longer chattered, and my eyes no longer tear. The water has stayed behind.

Breathe in. Breathe out.

Broken Hearts and Tragic Starts

by Meredith Lindsey

T he wind whipped my hair around my face, but I didn't bother combing it back. My eyes were shut to the world as I concentrated on breathing. *Inhale… Exhale…*

My lungs finally obeying, I tried to do as the online therapist suggested and focus on my sets of three. Three things I could smell: my strawberry shampoo as my hair tickled my nose, freshly mown grass, and overturned dirt. Three things I could hear: the leaves rustling in the trees behind me, a child crying as her mother tried to soothe her, and cars driving by in the afternoon traffic.

When I opened my eyes to find three things I could see though, my breath hitched in my chest once again. All I could see was the tombstone standing before me and the fresh mound of dirt where the rest of my heart was buried.

Roger Stone, the grave marker read. Beloved teacher, husband, and father. Below the inscription someone had added one final word. Murderer.

The black spray paint dripped in places, looking for all the world like dark, dried blood. I closed my eyes against the sight again, but the word was already branded on the back of my eyelids. I needed to wash them clean, but no matter how hard I squeezed my eyes the tears wouldn't come.

This wasn't how the world was supposed to work.

I was supposed to grow old and gray and have children of my own before putting my father in the ground, not as I was about to start my senior year of high school with my whole life ahead of me. He was supposed to drive me to college with my mother in tow and lecture me about parties and not accepting drinks from frat boys. He was going to walk me down the aisle one day and tell me how beautiful I looked in a white dress. He'd tell his grandchildren stories about me as he laughed at the photo albums filled with happy memories.

He wasn't supposed to replace those memories with this one dripping word painted harshly on his tombstone.

Voices carried across the cemetery, and I jumped as a hand grabbed my elbow.

"Come on, Cami," Michael urged, pulling me back towards the trees.

My friend had been giving me privacy, letting me grieve in peace, but now he beckoned me towards his car before the owners of the voices could come any closer.

It was too late, though. They'd already seen me. "Stone!" a girl screamed in our direction.

I turned towards the sound of my surname and flinched as the group of teens descended on us. Casey Lane was in the front of the pack, followed closely by her popular friends. I didn't have to guess why they were visiting the Plainfield Cemetery at the same time as me. I could see the fresh mounds of dirt and newly erected markers just three rows over from us. I knew what those gravestones read as well, only theirs had no reason to be vandalized.

Nathan Miles and Amelia Piper, two young souls whose time on this earth was cut so cruelly short. They were the picture-perfect couple, the cheerleading captain and football star who planned on finishing their last year of high school together before accepting admittance to a college where they would continue their perfect love story.

There would be no walk down the aisle for them either. Just a silent rest fifty yards away from the man who'd ended their lives.

"Need another drink, Camille?" another one of my classmates yelled at me. "We wouldn't want you to miss the opportunity to hit someone on your way home."

My feet were glued to the ground, but Michael managed to move me a second step back. It was as if my body welcomed the punishment these grieving kids promised.

"No, she'll wait until dark so she has a better chance at breaking up another happy couple. Their family can't kill just anyone."

They laughed as they drew closer, their faces cruel as they sized up their prey. It was easier to turn their emotions into hatred rather than accept the all-encompassing grief that came along with losing someone they loved. I would know. Blaming me for my father's actions was a temporary relief, but one they'd been obsessing over since that fateful night.

I finally allowed Michael to drag me along, turning my face away from their words.

"Going to take her to a liquor store, Varner?" another one sneered. "Maybe she can do us all a favor and run into a tree instead of the other lane of traffic!"

Their laughs echoed around my head as I escaped into the passenger seat of Michael's car. The door slammed, cutting off their taunts and encompassing me in blissful silence. But as he gunned the accelerator and sped away, I was faced with a new problem.

The car was suffocating.

We couldn't have been at the cemetery for more than twenty minutes, but that was plenty of time for Michael's black car to absorb all of the August heat. The air was thick, a solid thing that refused to go down my throat despite the air vents that were pumping it out in a steady, warm blast.

I didn't realize I was hyperventilating until I caught Michael moving to roll the windows down out of the corner of my eye. My vision was already starting to darken around the edges. As soon as the glass descended far enough, I shoved my head out the window like a dog. I welcomed the waves of fresh air and implored my stomach to settle down.

Don't throw up. Please don't throw up.

Ever since my father's death, I could barely stand to ride in a car for more than a few minutes. I had never suffered from claustrophobia before, but something about being enclosed in the same kind of vessel that my father and classmates had perished in immediately made my stomach roll. It was like I was trapped in my father's coffin, the warm air as stale and lifeless as my father's breath.

I inhaled deeply and leaned my head against the window frame. Michael squeezed my hand that lay limply in my lap but remained silent.

Michael Varner was the best friend I'd ever had. Neither of us were what you would call popular, but we'd avoided the negative attention of Plainfield High's hierarchy up to this point. Even now, after I'd been branded the daughter of a drunk driver and consequently a murderer, he stood by my side and tried to protect me from the heat. Sometimes I wondered if I deserved his friendship.

"It'll end soon," he said quietly.

I looked over at him and raised an eyebrow.

"Once you're out of town they'll stop bothering you. You can start fresh like your mom wants."

As if on cue, we pulled up beside my house where my mother was carrying a box that appeared entirely too heavy towards the back of the U-Haul. Michael threw the car in park and jumped out to lend a hand.

Cardboard boxes and plastic containers covered our tiny porch, and I made my way over to help as well. My chest tightened as I loaded the trailer with our belongings, but it had nothing to do with the physical exertion.

I tried to remind myself that this was a good thing. That my father wouldn't have wanted us to stay in a town where his daughter was bullied for his actions and his wife had to continue her teaching job as if he hadn't killed the older siblings of her elementary school students. I needed to convince myself that this was our best option, and that even though we were selling our home we would never leave the good memories of my father behind. There were plenty of good memories, too.

I remembered sitting on the porch in our rusted metal chairs, talking about our day while my mother cooked dinner. They were folded up and leaning against the side of the house now, wedged in by a group of boxes.

I remembered my dad catching his toe on the divot in our concrete driveway, the way his arms flailed before he tripped and fell into the grass. We'd made fun of him countless times for his clumsiness, and I smiled sadly at that divot as I stepped over it to load another box.

There were memories written and carved into every corner of our house. Good and bad, but memories all the same of what it was like to live with my entire family intact. I was glad my mother had gone to the trouble of moving everything outside so I wouldn't have to imagine my father walking through the door after another day at work.

How could one terrible mistake have the power to taint every good thing I remembered about him? Was I even allowed to grieve for a murderer?

My classmates would tell me no. But there was no way for me to explain that the actions of the man who died that night didn't define the person he was to me. He wasn't a useless drunk. He didn't live at the bar or come home wasted daily. He was my father, and there was so much more to him than the mistake that ended his life.

I had to hold onto those thoughts, because if I didn't, I was afraid that dark, inviting place in my mind might reach up and swallow me whole.

"I think we got it all," Michael announced as he shut and locked the trailer. I hadn't asked him to stay and help, but I was so grateful for his presence as I anticipated what happened next.

This was it. The official end of my life as I knew it.

I let Michael crush me in his arms and basked in the scent of Armani clinging to his T-shirt. I was going to miss this kid. I hoped once I was out of the picture the rest of our classmates would go back to ignoring him rather than the bullying that came with being the friend of a pariah. I knew we'd stay friends through texts and social media, but it was hard to let go of one of the last good things Plainfield had to offer.

I waited for my eyes to tear up, but the moisture never came. It felt like my emotions had been sealed off and buried along with the remains of my father. I didn't know when they would make it back to the surface.

I heard my mother's boots click across the concrete a moment before she threw her arms around both of us. The group hug lasted only a few seconds before I broke out of it, before their weight could become suffocating.

"Thanks for all your help, Michael." My mother patted him on the side of the face, probably because he was too tall for her to reach the top of his head. "You've been such a good friend to Camille. I know she's going to miss you."

I ducked my head so she couldn't see the pain in my eyes. Moving had been her decision, but I knew she didn't make it lightly. I didn't want her to feel guilty for doing what she thought was best for both of us.

"Of course, Terri." Michael grabbed my mother's hand as it rested against his face. "I hope you both find what you're looking for in Green Peaks."

I nodded silently. Green Peaks, Wyoming. It was all but a blip on the map, a small town encompassed by forests of trees and happened to be two hundred miles away. My Aunt Lacey and her husband lived there, and I knew my mom was hoping it could be the fresh start we both needed.

I wondered if the trees would be as suffocating as a car, or if all the nature would feel like freedom.

Michael extracted himself from my mother and gave me a quick peck on the cheek. He squeezed my shoulder one more time before opening the SUV's passenger door and waited for me to get in. The car was already running and blasting icy air. I rolled the window down as my mother climbed in beside me.

"Don't forget to text me when you've settled in," Michael reminded. "And try to get back to your painting, Cami. The world's an uglier place without your art."

I smiled and nodded. I hadn't gone near a paintbrush since my father's death, and I knew I'd have to face it eventually. My art had always been tied to my emotions, but until I could get past this numbness and feel things again, I didn't know how to channel my thoughts onto a canvas.

With my only good-bye behind us, I watched our home fade in the rearview mirror, blending into the identical houses of our subdivision. I'd probably never drive on this street again, and I couldn't bring myself to feel sad about it.

Every mile we drove took us farther away from the darkness of our past. I didn't know what the future would hold for me, but I could only hope that my life in Green Peaks would be the light at the end of the tunnel I'd been waiting for.

New beginnings so often start at the end of a tragic story. Like a phoenix rising from the ashes, I hoped this was the beginning of a new chapter in my life.

I wouldn't let grief have the final say. I could feel a pull in the direction we were going, as if this was exactly where I was meant to be.

If you want to continue Cami's story filled with magic, love, and murder, please check out Letters in the Attic *by Meredith Lindsey, available for purchase or free with Kindle Unlimited.*

Edited by Haley Kilgour

Talked Down

by H. C. Kilgour

I stare at the machine on the dashboard, willing myself to pick it up. My body is slow to react, like it's moving through molasses. No, it's resisting—self-preservation. It doesn't want what the mind needs.

Eventually my body wins over my mind, and I slump back into the seat, a frustrated cry escaping my lips. With my mouth open, tears manage to find an entrance back into my body. The salt stings, but it's the least of my hurts.

I try to grab the gun again, and my body fails to stop me this time. The metal is a fatal cool, harsh and unbecoming. As I work my fingers around the grip and lift it, I almost feel ashamed… at the weight of it… all.

My body, still yearning for life, refuses to let me hold the gun to my temple, to just end the misery. The gun pulls my hand into my lap, acting like an anchor tied to a sailor. Except the sailor will drown, my hand must yet commit its own end.

I know what I want. I've wanted it for so long. But my body refuses to admit defeat.

I have to do this. And do it I will.

I steel myself to fight my body once more and begin to lift the gun to my head. Time itself seems to slow, my body begging me to reconsider. But I won't. I can't.

Suddenly, there's a rap on the window and my head jerks towards the cause. There's a man outside—no, a police officer.

"Sir, is everything okay?" he calls.

I don't answer. It's night, the chances of him having a clear idea of what I'm trying to do is minimal. Then, there's a light, blinding. My pupils dilate and my eyes squint to subdue the brightness.

Now. I have to do it now.

My finger twitches on the trigger. *Just do it*, I tell myself. *Just do it!*

Another rap on the window and my finger freezes. I know how little pressure it would take. This could be over in less than a second.

"Mind if I come in?" the officer asks.

I don't answer and he takes this as an affirmative.

The car door creaks open ominously, like it's foretelling of horrors. With any luck, there's truth to it.

The officer isn't young, though neither is he old. But life… life has been lived. It's clear in the small blemishes and pocks of his face. The tiredness in his eyes. The gray flecking his hair.

With the door completely open, he shows me his hands. But why? It's not as if I intend him harm. No, the only one I'll ever harm again is myself.

Slowly, and cautiously, the officer eases himself into the passenger seat. Then, he closes the door. And none to quietly. The sound of metal on metal is like a gunshot. It hurts. But one actual bullet can stop that pain.

"I'm Victor. Victor Gregson. But my friends call me Juke," he says. His voice, there's something about the quiet timbre of it… it's soothing. It feels like he's been in my shoes. "What do they call you?"

"Carson," my throat manages to choke from me. My

body is still fighting, pleading for help. I can't let it.

The gun is still poised at my temple, but it's getting harder to hold there. The gun, it seems to weigh so much, even if I know it's hardly anything.

"Carson," Juke says thoughtfully, "I used to work with a guy named Carson."

Used to. In Juke's line of work, I'm willing to bet he's dead. Just like I should be. Will be.

Juke settles into the seat, as if we're going on a long drive. "He's a detective now. Great guy."

Fate spared the other Carson. I almost want to laugh. Maybe once I'm dead I can live vicariously through him.

"Just like I know you're a great guy," he continues. "So, tell me, why are you here, sonny?"

I choke on a laugh, feeling like hands are around my neck strangling the sound. Any reminiscence of something other than this will defeat the purpose of the gun. I can't let that happen.

Juke doesn't seem off put by my manic laugh; he seems completely unaffected in fact. Then I notice a kind of sorrow wash over him. The kind of sorrow that breaks a stranger's heart. The kind that breaks mine.

I can feel my hand beginning to shake, beginning to waver—body over mind.

"Well, if you're not going to tell me why you're here, I guess I'll just have to tell you," Juke says.

He hasn't looked at me since getting in the car, hasn't tried to take the gun, or even touch me—and he doesn't start now. But his voice, somehow, I can feel it, taking my free hand and squeezing it, placing itself on the barrel of the gun and pushing it away from my head, staring me in the eyes and telling me this is the wrong choice.

"You're here because you think you've had enough." He doesn't bother to ask me if he's right; he knows he is. "You've seen and done things no one your age should have. And now you feel alone. Afraid. And you think this is your only choice."

"It is," I manage to say, the gun sliding into my lap, ready to spring to action—if I can defeat my body again.

"It's not." I expect to feel scolded, but I don't. It's almost like he's opened the door to another choice… but there can't be another choice.

"Mind if I tell you a bit about myself?" Juke asks.

Again, my silence is taken for affirmation.

"I came from the bad side of Philly. I'm talking gangs, drugs, you name it, I saw it. All before the age of ten. Hell, I joined in most the time."

No one should have that kind of childhood. I pity him. But, clearly, he's managed to escape hell. I'd tried, but I was stuck too fast. I was stuck in quicksand and trying to get out only killed me faster.

"I was… oh, I must've been eighteen or so. I was out on the streets more often than not. See, dad was a drug dealer with no time for me. I was addicted to what dad was selling and, finally, I'd had enough."

A heaviness sat on Juke's shoulders now. Had he… I almost dare not ask myself that question.

"I knew how much I could take. And I knew how much I need to slip into oblivion, high out of my mind."

"What stopped you?" I couldn't say what made me ask the question, but I needed to know. What had made him think life was worth living?

"Who," he corrected. "I was too doped out to recognize him… see, I was already high. He found me in the local crack house. You only went in there if you wanted to be left alone. More than one person had crawled in there hoping to die."

"Who was he?"

"Never got a name," Juke said, shaking his head like it was the greatest shame in the world. "I think he was some old man who lived on the block. But he crawled into the house after me and found me with a needle in my arm, ready to push the plunger."

"Why didn't you?"

"The old man talked to me," Juke said. "Told me about himself. Then he listened to me. So, tell me about yourself?"

I couldn't place it, but I was… comfortable with this man. I… trusted him. The first words were the hardest to say. I'd seen so many awful things in Iraq… lost so many friends. But as I talked about each wound, I could feel them beginning to heal. Not completely, but the process had started.

By the time I was done talking, it was all I could do to cry let alone pull the trigger. I didn't know what I had to live for, but there was something out there.

"And that's my story, Ava," I say, leaning on the railing of the bridge. The water below is far, yet it is still, offering a sense of tranquility. Something I know the girl wishes for.

Ava's still on the other side, her knuckles white against the black paint. I can see her throat bobbing as it attempts to keep her silent.

"So, tell me about yourself?"

The Mirror

by H. C. Kilgour

I look in the mirror.
I see what the world sees.
I see everything I'm not.

I see my layers.
Rolls on my belly.
Handles on my hips.
Back aching boulders on my chest.
Cellulite on my thighs.

I see what the world sees.
I see everything I'm not.
I see I'm not enough.

How can I be when I don't wear a size 2?
How can I be when every part of me jiggles when I walk?
How can I be when I'm not fit like the other girls?
How can I be when I can be weighed in stones?

I look in the mirror.
I see what the world sees.
I see everything I'm not.

Shadows of the Mind

≠≠≠

I look in the mirror.
I see what the world sees.
I see everything I'm not.

I see all my blemishes.
The pimples on my forehead and nose.
The acne scars on my cheeks.
The pale skin that no one finds attractive.

I see what the world sees.
I see everything I'm not.
I see I'm not enough.

How can I be when a perfect sun kissed bronze in unattainable?
How can I be when I can't turn back time for wrinkles and scars?
How can I be when I smile, and my teeth don't light up the room?
How can I be when makeup makes no sense?

I look in the mirror.
I see what the world sees.
I see everything I'm not.

≠≠≠

I look in the mirror.
I see what the world sees.
But do I?
I see everything I could be.

A little bit of makeup goes a long way, my mom says.
My lashes seem full and eye-catching with mascara. But who pays attention to that?
The foundation helps hide my acne scars. But they're still there. Who am I kidding?
The eye shadow draws attention to my eyes. Better people look there than elsewhere.

I see what the world sees.
I see everything I could be.
I see I'm not enough.

How can I be when I can't do a perfect cat eye?
How can I be when the color of my face doesn't match the rest of my body?
How can I be when a pretty face doesn't fix a flabby body?
How can I be when a personality isn't enough?

I look in the mirror.
I see what the world sees.
But do I?
I see everything I could be.

≠≠≠

I look in the mirror.
I see what the world sees.
I see what I can become with a bit of work.
I see everything I could be.

Go to the gym. You'll lose the weight. I'm trying but it's hard.
Eat healthier. You'll lose the weight. I'm trying but it's

hard.
Eat less. You'll lose weight. I'm trying but it's hard.

Get nicer clothes. You'll feel good when you look good.
I'm trying but it's hard.
Have a skin care routine. You'll look years younger. I'm
trying but it's hard.
Teeth whitening strips. They worked wonders for me.
I'm trying but it's hard.

I see what the world sees.
I see everything I can become with a bit of work.
I see I'm not enough.

How can I be when my pants are looser, but I still look
the same?
How can I be when I can't afford the healthy stuff?
When it only tastes good drowned in butter and cheese?
How can I be when the clothes make me self-conscious?
Good clothes are tight, tailored. But that just means they
show everything off. Everything I'm uncomfortable
with.
How can I be when I still have scars and wrinkles?
How can I be when the strips only work for a day?

I look in the mirror.
I see what the world sees.
I see everything I can be with a bit of work.
I see everything I could be.

≠≠≠

I look in the mirror.
He shows me what he sees.

I try to see what he sees.

Men say the like super model skinny. But I like you. I like that there's more of you to hold. To love.
I like your laugh lines and crows' feet. They help me remember the fun times we've had.
You've got acne scars. So do I. And other scars from being a dumb kid.
I don't want someone pretty to look at. I want someone to share a life with.

I try to see what he sees.
I really do.
But it's hard to not see what the world sees too.
I see I'm not enough.

How can I be when he could have any girl he wanted?
How can I be when the world still sees the wrinkles?
When they tell me I look old.
How can I be when his scars have stories? They make him more rugged. They add to his allure.
How can I be when he has to put up with this?

I look in the mirror.
He shows me what he sees.
I try to see what he sees.
I see everything I'm not.

≠≠≠

I look in the mirror.
It's been a while, old friend.
How long has it been since I stopped caring what you thought?

Shadows of the Mind

I see what I see.

I see a woman.
Healthy.
Yes, I'm not a size 2. But who cares?!
Yes, I'm not a size 2. But the food was worth it.
Yes, I'm not a size 2. But most people aren't.
Yes, I'm not a size 2. But *I* don't care.

I see a woman.
Beautiful.
I have laugh lines and wrinkles. Well, duh. That happens when you laugh a lot.
Well, duh. It means I've had a good life.
Well, duh. We all get old.
Well, duh, I'm beautiful. I know it and damn anyone who says I'm not.

I see a woman.
Successful.
I have a beautiful family. And I wouldn't trade them for the world.
I have a job I love. And that's something special.
I have people who care about me. And they know I love them back.
Success is subjective. I won't compare myself to others.

I see what I see.
I see everything I am.
I see I am enough.

I look in the mirror.
For a moment I see what the world sees.
But the world's opinion doesn't matter anymore.

I see what I see.
I see me.

I see wonderful, beautiful me.
I see I am enough.

I see we are all enough.

Grief is Only the Beginning of the Journey

My Story: Based on True Events
by Laura Lukasavage

The saying couldn't be more accurate. A parent should never have to bury their child, but a child should never have to bury their parents before the child has grown and had them by their side for the most important milestones in life. My mother missed them all.

June 4th, 2005

Groggily I shifted onto my side on my old, tan, flower covered couch, a light moan of annoyance escaping my lips as the bright light hit my closed eyelids. My friend Ashley kept calling to me, but my eyes refused to open, the morning crust holding my lashes prisoner.

"Laura, you need to get up, there are cops in your house," Ashley whispered.

My heart stopped as my eyes pried themselves open. I popped into a seated position so fast my head felt funny.

I glanced around the room and, sure enough, a tall, dark, young man in his black and blue uniform stood on the other side of the room. His eyes connected with mine. He forced a smile and walked into the hall heading toward me and my sister's room, the bathroom, and my mother and stepfather's room.

I lived in a small apartment in Brooklawn, New Jersey. It wasn't the best place, but it was home, and I wouldn't have had it any other way.

My early childhood was spent with my grandparents —my mother's parents—until I was six and she came to take me back to live with her. She'd struggled with a lot of mental health issues, which made it hard for her to be the mother she hoped to be. But she took the time she needed to be the parent I deserved and for the past eight years I'd finally felt at home.

My mother and I were thick as thieves; she was my best friend—no offense to any of my then four best friends. There was just this bond we shared that no one could match. She was the reason I had these friends to begin with. I've always been shy, but my mother was the opposite. When she saw a little girl playing outside when we first moved into the apartment, she yelled out and asked if I could play with her. Her name was Tammy, and she was one of my closest friends.

"Laura, what should we do?" Alexis asked from the carpeted floor.

Alexis and Ashley are sisters, Alexis being the elder.

"I'll going to go find out what's going on," I replied.

"Do you want us to wait?" Ashley asked.

I shook my head. "No, you guys go home. I'll call you later."

They shared a look before turning back to me, worry and skepticism on their faces.

I smiled. "I promise. It'll be fine."

I walked them to the door and once it clicked shut, I headed down the hall to find two officers standing in front of my parents' door.

"Excuse me," I mumbled as I tried to move past them into the bedroom.

The younger officer just looked at me sadly.

The other moved into a better position to block me from entering. "I'm sorry, you can't go in there right now."

"Why not?"

"Your parents asked me to have you get yourself and your sister ready to go to your grandparents. They'll be here shortly to pick you up," he responded.

"I would like to talk to my mother first."

The younger cop spoke, "I'm sorry but you can't. Please, go wake your sister. They'll be here any minute."

Annoyed, I moved past them, opening my bedroom door. I closed it behind me as my eyes fixed on my four-year old sister, passed out on the bottom bunk. I heard voices in the hall as the doorbell rang. Sighing I went to wake her up.

"Your grandparents are here," one of the cops called.

Christina wiped the sleep from her eyes. A smile spread over her face as her eyes connected with mine. We also have a deep bond despite being almost ten years apart. Hearing our grandparents' voices, she rushed past me, pulling the door open and heading for the front door. Walking past my parents' room, a feeling of dread filled my stomach, the unknown eating away slowly at my sanity.

Everyone remained quiet during the car ride to my grandparents' house in Mount Ephraim. That house gives me nightmares, haunting my dreams even when I no longer live under its roof. But that's a story for another day.

The seconds ticked by slowly, filling the silence with a cold embrace of unanswered questions. Seconds turned to minutes and minutes turned to hours as the pit in my stomach grew.

Denial

My grandmother's stiff tone filled the quiet living room. "Laura, Pop-pop wants to speak with you. He's in our room."

I stood, my body taking over where my mind couldn't. Everything up to that moment had been torture but with each step down the hall my heart beat louder in my ears and one thing remained in the front of my mind —my grandfather never talks to me alone unless it's bad news.

On the car ride to their house, the only thing I'd asked was why I couldn't talk with my mom. Was she ok? What was going on? I received this answer: Your mom is fine. She's going to the hospital. I had pushed for more but received nothing further.

I found Pop-pop sitting on his bed, lost in thought. I sat down next to him quietly. Waiting.

"Laura, this morning something happened to your mom," he started.

I remained silent waiting for him to continue. The minutes ticked on.

"She's gone," he whispered.

"Gone?"

"She passed away before you woke up this morning."

I stood in a fast, aggressive manner, heat rising to

my face, my chest contracting as pain flooded in.

"What are you talking about? You said she was going to the hospital. You told me she was fine," I practically growled.

"We didn't know how to tell you," he said, not looking at me. He stood and reached out for me.

I pulled back. "You lied to me." My voice cracked as the pain in my chest increased and tears filled my eyes.

I had never seen my grandfather look so old, broken, and lost. The vibrant man I knew was gone, his world shattered with the death of his oldest and only daughter. And just like him, I felt the walls closing in, crumbling on top of me as it got harder to breathe.

He took another step forward, sending me darting from the room. I slammed my great-grandmother's bedroom door closed behind me, sending the lock on the back of the knob into place before taking a step backward.

"Laura," my grandfather said my name in a broken voice.

I moved into a fetal position on the bed as the truth washed over me in an unforgiving wave. I struggled to breathe as cries filled the room. It took me a moment to realize they were mine as warm tears escaped my eyes, staining the pillow beneath my face. My body shook uncontrollably with the forcefulness of my cries, as I felt my heart shatter into pieces inside my heaving chest. In that moment, I understood what is meant when they say someone can die from a broken heart. I found myself wishing for death, because a life without my mother, without my best friend, wasn't a life I wanted to live. Heat filled my body as I looked to the ceiling, imagining it was the night sky.

Anger

"You bring her back, you hear me! You bring her back or you take me too," I yelled at my invisible God.

Being Catholic has always been a part of me, but in that moment, I found myself hating everything about it. I prayed this was only a dream, a nightmare, and that I would wake up in a world where my mother hadn't been taken from me. I sobbed until my energy was spent and I fell into a deep sleep.

The next morning brought the same heartbreak, and I didn't leave bed. I didn't eat. I only cried, slept, and repeated. Monday morning came and, in a zombie-like fashion, I pulled on my polo, pulled up my knee-high socks, and headed to the car.

My grandfather drove me to school in silence, telling me he would be there to pick me up at the end of the day. I felt everyone's eyes on me as they whispered. Some offered their sincere condolences. I ignored them all, making my way through the week in daze.

Eighth grade graduation was around the corner, along with our New York field trip and the dinner dance. The thought of graduation or starting high school weighed my mind. My mother and I had been talking, planning for this, like most things in my life. We'd had my sweet sixteen and twenty first birthday all planned out. We'd even had my children's names picked. Isabella and David. There was nothing we didn't talk about and now it was all down the drain. I didn't want to do any of it. No first boyfriend, no high school, no more birthdays. My life ceased to exist the moment she took her final breath.

Bargaining

My eyes followed each person as they walked past,

offering their condolences to me and their goodbyes to my mother. Me, I was rooted in place, afraid to approach the coffin; it was the last place I wanted to see my mother.

I watched Mom-mom as she cried in Pop-pop's arms. I knew he was holding it together on the outside, but on the inside was broken and hollow, hiding in the shadows—like me. My eyes caught my great-grandmother's as she approached the coffin. Steps away she fell to the ground with an agonizing wail. Everyone rushed to her side, helping her to her feet as the sobs continued to escape this woman whom I'd never seen cry before.

Mom-mom turned to me when Pop-pop left to help my great-grandmother back to her seat. Her tone was filled with distaste as she asked, "What's wrong with you?"

Unsure of what she meant, I remained silent.

My silence caused her to continue her assault. "You're acting like it's a party now that your mother's dead."

Surprised at her words, I was about to refute her as Pop-pop returned. Instead, I chose to remain silent, knowing this was simply a stage of grief Mom-mom needed to go through.

Moments later, Mom-mom nudged my arm. "Go say goodbye to your mother. Give her a kiss."

My eyes widened with fear. I had been dreading this moment. I had planned on not touching her, fearing how cold she would feel and how final the goodbye would be. My grandparents forced me up to my mother's side, and I gazed down at someone I knew was my mother but looked nothing like her. She was heavier, swollen, and her face didn't look the same.

My eyes began to sting but I pushed down the tears once more as Pop-pop's words reached my ears. "Give her a kiss goodbye. They need to take the body to the cemetery."

Always wishing to please my grandfather, I did the one thing every cell in my body was fighting against. I bent over to place a light kiss upon her ice-cold cheek. It is a feeling and image that, even after twenty years, still haunts me.

It wasn't until I sat next to my stepfather in a church pew as Amazing Grace sounded that I couldn't hold back anymore. The floodgates opened wide as my cheeks became the home of the waterfall that made its way down my cheeks. My stepfather's arm tightened around me as I cried into his chest, our bodies shaking in unison from the severity of our sorrow. One event rolled into the next as I watched them lower my mother into the ground. I stood in the background, a statue, like someone looking in on another person's life.

Depression

The following events of my life moved along but were clouded and taken over by my sorrow. Even today, I can't recall my eighth-grade graduation. Starting high school lifted my spirits slightly, as I knew it was a fresh start in the sense no one knowing me or the most recent events that had taken place in my life. No one looked at me with doe eyes or was unsure of what to say. It was also a chance to make genuine friends, as I really hadn't had any in school before this point.

With high school came many temptations and since my mind was full of only despair and anger, I was willing to go down the rabbit hole if it meant being numb to the pain, even if only for a little while. I fell into the world most teenagers find themselves in at one point or another. I took up smoking cigarettes, drinking liquor, partying, smoking weed, Xanax, cutting, and the dating scene. I threw myself into anything that would make me feel different. Whatever washed over the pain I welcomed with open arms, even if it brought on a whole new source of pain. But I preferred the heartbreak of my relationships over the crippling devastation the thoughts of my mother brought. So, I continued on this path for most of my teenage years.

I was swallowed by the empty void my mother's absence had left.

I was lucky I wasn't up arrested or, honestly, didn't wind up dead. It took most of high school before I took a look at myself and knew this person wasn't who I was or who I wanted to be. And it definitely wasn't someone my mother would be proud of. I had made her a promise not even a week before her passing, which, for the most part, I had kept. She'd made me promise to never do drugs, and not to grieve. Other than the drinking, weed, and occasional Xanax, I had kept that part of my promise.

I placed myself in relationships with men who were broken and damaged, their inner selves mirroring my own. Part of me did it because I blamed myself for my mother's death and I wanted to be hurt.

Years before she died, I woke up feeling something wasn't right, and I begged her to let me stay home from school; she talked my stepdad into letting me remain home. A few hours later, someone called but I told them my mom was sleeping. Once I hung up, I went to go check on her. I don't know how I knew to check but I placed my hand under her nose and noticed she was barely breathing. I called the cops, and they came. I overheard them talking with Mom-mom, telling her that if someone had called an hour later it would've been too late. I wasn't supposed to be home for hours. I'd saved my mother that day but hadn't felt there was anything extraordinary about it at the time and had had a sleepover that weekend.

I begged and pleaded with God to bring her back to me, that I would do anything, but he never listened.

Acceptance

Now, nineteen years later, I have finally healed. Don't get me wrong, there are still hard days where I cry and my heart hurts and I wish she were here. But most days are good and when I think of her, I smile. I also know that without her loss I wouldn't have become the person I am today. I might never have picked up books in high school to get lost in. I know I never would have written poems to try to be closer to her. I don't think I would have discovered my love for writing. I wouldn't understand the hurt of the world, at least not as young as I did.

It molded me to better understand the world of pain, loss, and grief and to connect with others. Even if I would never want this kind of pain to be experienced by anyone. It also made me want to share my journey and to help others who have walked the same road. To help them get to a place of peace long before I did.

I want my books to do for my readers what J. K. Rowling and Stephanie Meyer did for me. They gave me a world to get lost in when my grief was at an all-time high, gave me a place to hide and something to fall in love with again. Books opened me up to a new world and helped me find my place along with grounding me. I want my readers to not only crave my next story, but I want those suffering from loss, abuse, bullying, or self-doubt to be able to read my books and gain insight and hope from the pages I have created.

My journey has been far from easy, and I miss my mother, and so many others, every day. But today I can say I can breathe again. I have come to a place where it doesn't always hurt my heart when the thought of my mother and those I've lost crosses my mind.

Loss is a part of life we cannot escape. But it is how we grieve, move on, and continue to live our lives that matters in the end.

Drifting Away
by David F. Balog

"Where are you right now?" Jane asked, squeezing my shoulder.

I was staring up at the three white, fluffy clouds blemishing an otherwise clear sky, while listening to the river splash and flow. The breeze was light, causing the clouds to slowly change. The one that caught my attention looked like a bunny, then a beetle. Then the cloud turned gray and transformed into some Lovecraftian horror with tentacles reaching for the next cloud, waiting to draw it into its gaping maw.

"Hmm?" I responded, shaking my head as I was drawn back to reality. "I felt like I was floating down the river. It… it was calling to me. I can still feel it pulling me away." I looked down into the water. White patches of bubbles swirled before me, cascading over the edge onto the rocks below. The sound of it was soothing yet disquieting.

Jane put an arm around me as tears welled in my eyes. *Why am I like this?* I asked myself. *Why do I do this every time?*

It was a gorgeous May afternoon—warm, sunny, dry. We were on a walk through the woods, the smell of pine filling the air, following the creek until it came to the falls. Jane and I sat along the edge, had a picnic next to the waterfall, and kissed. A lot.

Even in my happiest moments, the depression comes out of nowhere.

"What would happen if you allowed it to sweep you away?" she asked. She wasn't a therapist, but could have been. Jane had a talent for asking leading questions.

"I don't know. I would probably drown eventually. It's like a siren's call. I just want to drift away, to disappear."

She rubbed my back in slow circles. "Anything in particular you want to disappear from?"

"No. Yes. I don't know. I love you. I do, but I'm not happy here."

"Here with me? The park?"

I waved my hands around, careful not to hit her. "No, here. This world. My life. Everything sucks. Too many wars, crazy politicians, Earth is dying... I don't see a future. I don't know which is worse, growing up during the Cold War and constantly waiting for a nuclear strike, or watching kids practicing in case someone comes into their classroom to shoot them. We're all doomed. My job sucks. Hell, I could barely afford this lunch. I know you love me, but I can't fathom why. You deserve so much more. You're all I've got, and I'll eventually push you away," I ranted.

Jane held me as I wept, keeping her thoughts private until I had calmed. "You're overwhelmed. Let's take this in small pieces, okay?" She kissed me, but all I could taste were my tears.

Jane hugged me, squeezing against my ribs. "First of all, I'm not going anywhere, so you can put that worry out of your head. Secondly, there's not much we can do about the world at large. At least, not right now. So can you put that aside?" she asked as she stepped back, keeping her hands on the sides of my chest.

"I guess," I sniffed. "It's hard though."

"I know. You said that you would drown. Is that what you want?"

"Not particularly," I said. "It's not a great way to die. I'm certainly not going to jump over the falls. That would just be painful. Probably break a few bones, but it's not likely to kill me outright."

"And you think about dying?" she prodded.

"Sometimes. I've considered different ways, but I don't think I could do it myself. Probably. I want something peaceful, to just fall asleep and never wake up again. I thought about walking over the lake next time it ices over. I've heard that freezing is like falling asleep. I would be gone before anyone realized it, and the lake would claim my body so no one would have to spend the money to cremate me." I sighed as a tear dropped from her eye. "I'm not suicidal, just apathetic. I know it would hurt you, and my family, but if it was something that just happened, I wouldn't argue.

"Years ago, on a high school field trip, I contemplated jumping out the window. We were on the tenth floor, and I figured it was high enough to kill me on impact. While I sat in the hotel room crying, I don't remember if there was any reason, but probably because I hadn't slept the whole trip. I have trouble sleeping in new places surrounded by strangers. Anyway, one of my roommates came in. I didn't know the guy—we didn't share any classes—but I poured my heart out to him. Fortunately, he was very kind, listening to me like you are, and didn't make fun of me or anything. He eventually coaxed me out of the room to sit with the rest of the group."

Jane cried as I lost myself in her hazel, gold-flecked

eyes. "Maybe he was sent to the room by an angel."

"Maybe. Who knows? I don't discount the possibility, but I don't think anyone's watching out for me. After Susan died, I lost whatever tenuous connections I had to the spirit realm, though I look at you sometimes and wonder." I smiled.

"Oh, I'm no angel." She smiled wickedly, baring her teeth and wiggling her eyebrows.

I laughed. "Either way, I'm lucky we found each other." I leaned forward and kissed her. "I never wanted to be here," I continued. "I've never felt comfortable in this life, like I belonged. When I was a baby, mom used to call me her 'changeling' because I didn't cry and fuss as much as she expected me to. Maybe part of that stuck with me. Maybe I am a changeling, a fairy child swapped for a human one. I don't belong here."

"Well, I for one am glad you are here. My life wouldn't be the same without you." Jane stuck her hand over my mouth before I could protest. "You make me happy. Happier than I've been in a long time. Don't you dare try to take that away from me."

I licked her hand, and she pulled away, laughing, as she wiped it on her pants. "Me too. At least, most of the time." I shook my head. "I don't know why I do this. I ruin everything."

"It's okay. It happens. We all have our moments."

"It's not just moments for me," I said calmly, though I wanted to scream. I was starting to get angry. At myself. And I held back because I didn't want to be angry with her. "Happiness is in moments, depression is my default state."

"Have you tried talking to a professional? I love you, but I can only do so much."

I threw my hands up. "How can I afford a therapist?

Where would I find the time if I could? I can't afford to take off work, and they'll just prescribe me 'happy pills'. That's all doctors do anymore. 'Here, take these, they'll make you all better. Don't worry about getting addicted or the side effects, we have pills for those too!',” I mocked.

"It's not really like that, you know," she chided.

"I know. I don't know if it's brain chemistry, or a hormonal imbalance, or just the way my brain is designed. Whatever it is, I've been this way my whole life. Depression is my normal. Talking doesn't fix that. It's just saying it out loud and making it more real. It doesn't get it out of my head."

"I'm sorry," she frowned. It's always cute the way she sticks out her bottom lip like that.

"And this is why I don't like to talk about it. People get 'sad for me'. It upsets people, then I have to pretend I'm feeling better to make *them* feel better. This is why when people ask me how I'm doing, I say 'Great!' or 'I'm doing well'. No one wants to hear how I really feel. It makes them uncomfortable. The closest I can usually get is 'It's a long story' and no one ever follows up."

"I can see that. It makes sense why you wouldn't say anything to just anybody, but we're a couple. Don't you trust me?"

"I do. Of course, I do!" I kissed her for a couple seconds. "That's not the point. I don't want you to feel bad for me or get uncomfortable because I'm in a sad mood. I'm afraid I'll drive you away when you can't take it anymore eventually. I've been hiding it my whole life. I'm pretty good at it by now."

"Burying it is not the same as dealing with it. You can only push it down for so long."

"True. That's why we're having this conversation." I

chuckled without mirth.

"Seriously, I'm worried about you," Jane pressed.

"And this is why I didn't want to have this discussion. I have to control my feelings, so I don't make others feel bad. Now you are worried, and you will always feel this way when you think about me. It happens every time."

"That's not all I feel. Yes, this adds to it, but I still think you're wonderful. There's a lot more to you than your depressive moods. I hate to be cliché but look at the positive. You have a home, a loving family, me, a cute butt," she said as she slapped my rump.

"Hey! I'm more than a sex object, I´ll have you know."

"Yes, you are. A lot more. I know it can be hard to see that sometimes, and that's okay. We all get upset over the state of the world; there's a lot to be angry about. But there's good too. You can't worry about everything. You know the saying about control, right?"

I shook my head.

She straightened her back and held up her head, as if she were about to give a speech. "Ain't no use in worryin," she smiled, dipping into a southern accent, "whether you got control or you ain't. If you got control, ain't nothin' to worry about. And if you don't, then don't worry 'cause you ain't in control."

We laughed together. It felt nice. For a moment.

"Most of the time, it feels more like National Lampoon's *Deteriorata*," I said.

"I'm not familiar with that."

"You are a fluke of the universe," I sang. "You have no right to be here. Whether you can hear it or not, the universe is laughing behind your back."

"It does feel that way sometimes, doesn't it?" She

laughed.

I should have laughed too. Though it's supposed to be a comedy track, it still hits close to home. I've had that issue since my wife died. It's been over three years, and I still can't get past it. All music sounds like it's in a minor key, and lyrics have different meanings now. Breakup songs imply death, and even cheerful ones feel off. *Over the Rainbow*, for example, feels like a suicide song; my wife "flew over the rainbow, so why, oh why can't I?"

Being with Jane these past few months has taken some of that sting away, but the grief is always there. Combined with my natural inclination towards depression, it's been hard to move forward. I've sabotaged friendships and relationships before, and I can see it happening again. I want to be open and honest with those I care about, but usually when they find out how broken I am, they drift away. I never understood why it never happened with Susan, but it was probably because she was a lot like me.

We both preferred being alone and quiet. Most evenings, we would sit on the couch and read or play games next to each other, usually with me rubbing her ice-cold feet at the same time. Susan and I did everything together: chores, errands, cooking, *everything*. More often than not, she prodded me into action, deciding when things were to be done. This included the many instances where she desired a treat, usually cookies, and wanted me to make them for her. Then it was my turn to get her off the couch and make them with me. We made a good team. Now, I do everything alone, which was easier before we met. Now, there's always something missing.

"Let's focus on you right now, okay," Jane said,

bringing my attention back.

I nodded.

"I know you aren't happy with work. Why don't you try somewhere else?"

"I have," I sighed. "I've applied for other jobs, but I haven't gotten any call backs. I hear on the news how everyone is looking for help, but I can't make them bring me in for an interview. I don't know what to do. I'm smart, well-educated, devastatingly handsome—" I swaggered, "—but no one seems to want me. I'm just killing time, and it's killing me."

"When we get home, let me look at your resume, okay?" she asked. "Maybe I can help you fix it. I can try to help you find something that will better suit you."

"Yeah, but at my age, it's unlikely." I shook my head. "Every place wants someone younger, that they can mold into whatever they want them to be. I've been out of school for too long, can't find anything that fits my degree, and can't afford to start at the bottom again."

"You can always ask me to help," she said, looking into my eyes. "You know that, right."

"I guess."

"But…"

"But I feel like you do so much for me already," I sighed, tears forming again. "I never do anything for you."

"You planned this hike. You picked this park, chose the route, packed a delicious lunch. You do a lot for me."

"Parks are free," I grumbled, "and it's just sandwiches, chips, and pop."

"And little almond cookies!" She clapped and squealed. "I can tell these are homemade."

"Yeah, but those are simple." I shrugged. Cooking is something that always used to bring me joy, but all my recipes are for more than one person. Before meeting Jane, I would have leftovers for a full week. Susan and I were a great team in the kitchen; Jane… not so much, but she tries.

"Hey, do I look like I need anything fancy?" she laughed. "I'm with you because I love you, not for what you can or can't give me. Well, maybe one thing," she whispered, then nibbled on my ear.

I laughed and pushed her away. "That tickles!"

She stepped forward and hugged me. I hugged her back, trying not to squeeze her too hard.

I began to cry again.

"Hey, hey, shh. I've got you," she whispered.

"But why?" I asked. "You could do so much better. Someday you're going to realize that and leave me behind." I knew even as I said it that it was a self-fulfilling prophecy.

She continued to hold me until I calmed again. "I love you. You're sweet, kind, gentle, loving, devastatingly handsome," she mimicked, shifting her shoulders. "I don't care about what you can buy for me, whether we go for a walk in the park and not on an expensive cruise. I *like* the park. You bring me joy. That's all I want from you." She kissed me.

This time I could taste more than my tears as our lips parted and our tongues met.

"Mmm, root beer!" she smiled, licking her lips.

"You're silly," I chuckled. "I love you. How do you put up with me?"

Jane blinked. "I thought you were the one putting up with me!"

We packed up the picnic and held hands as we walked back to the car in silence. Jane was right about focusing on what I can control and not fretting about the rest. Knowing it, believing it, and practicing it are entirely different things, however. We listened to the radio on the way back to her house while I contemplated my feelings.

Despite occasional moments of joy with Jane, the depression is always there. I distract myself with entertainments—books, television, games, hobbies. I haven't done any embroidery or woodworking in a while, mostly because my time is taken up with my writing. They help while I'm focused on them. It might make me appear lazy to others, as I'm not 'accomplishing anything' according to society's work ethic, which also dings my self-esteem, but they're the only thing that seems to help. It doesn't solve the problem, but neither has anything else I've tried.

I refuse to fall to drugs or alcohol; I've lost too many friends and family that way. Those things never help, but gods, I crave their numbing qualities. I wish there were a healthier way to oblivion.

Part of me blames our culture. We're not allowed to feel as we do. Unless you present as happy, or at least content, then you are stigmatized and ostracized. How many of us are hiding? How many are denying our natural state? There are limits, I cannot argue that. Despite my desires to be left alone and hide away forever, I can still function in society, playing the game and pretending. I often wonder if depression is normal and it's the happy people that are the odd ones. At least that would make me feel less alone.

Is that where the line is?

My desire to die is not the same as being actively suicidal. I'm glad that help is available for those seeking a path to avoid going that far, though it is, of course, understaffed since it's not really a governmental priority.

Every night I hope to not wake up the next morning, and am continuously disappointed by still being here, but that is as far as I'm willing to go.

"I had a nice time today," said Jane as we reached her door. "I'm sorry that you feel down, and I understand that it's how you feel. I'm not going to invalidate your feelings or tell you to cheer up. But I do want you to know that I am here, and I love you. I want you to be happy. I want to make you happy. I also want you to be true to yourself. If you're going to change, change for you, not for me. Okay?"

"Okay." I kissed and hugged her. "Thank you. For listening, for understanding. I appreciate it and you. You're amazing."

"I am, aren't I?" She laughed. "Maybe wisdom comes with age after all."

I chuckled. "I can only hope. It's the only chance I have left!"

We kissed again and went inside. Though the deeper sadness still sat in my heart, I found that I could once again find contentment. Sometimes, even joy.

Solitude

by David F. Balog

Solitude.
I had long wished for quietude.
And now regret my foolishness.
Wishes never come true in the way we want.

Solitude.
The shards of my broken heart
Cut whenever I pick them up,
Bleeding tears from my core.

Solitude.
This plague has taken so much,
From so many, for so long.
I have little left to lose.

She's gone.
Taken by disease.
It stole her from me.
A thief hidden within her,
Took my most valuable treasure.

Solitude.
How do I live? *Why* do I live?
Why continue when all I lived for is gone?

Surviving is a curse.

Solitude.
I'm not suicidal, just lost,
Heartbroken and apathetic,
Suffering from her loss, uncaring about myself.

She's gone.
Our lives were deeply intertwined,
Yet we kept our individuality and independence.
My heart is frayed as I unravel from her.

Solitude.
I reach across the couch, the bed,
One hand outstretched into empty air,
The other stifling my unending flow of tears.

She's gone.
Though I'm lonely, I'm never alone.
Friends share their sympathy and empathy,
But cannot fill the abyss left by her passing.

She's gone.
A scrapbook found,
Containing dreams deferred and talents atrophied;
Secrets never shared, a life unlived.
A life that now cannot be lived.

Solitude.
Accounts go untold without her to share them with.
We shall both carry our stories unto death,
Neither of us knowing our full lives.

Shadows of the Mind

She's gone.
A house full of stuff,
Every room, every decoration is her,
A constant reminder of her passing.

Solitude.
I face the world with lies.
A brave face and smile to disguise the pain,
Pain that no one wants me to share. Not any more.

Solitude.
Religious talk and empty words,
Offered to uplift my painful burden.
Surrender stifles growth, capitulation smothers healing.

She's gone.
Yet I carry her mark:
Her name and print indelibly inscribed in my soul.
Her name and print indelibly over my heart. forever.

Solitude.
Empty hangers in the closets where her cardigans once
hung.
Shoes with no feet to fill them.
Her presence is even felt in this void.

Solitude.
I no longer find joy in our shared tasks.
Our creative endeavors have become chores.
The chores are now impositions.

Solitude.
I see you in my sleep,
For it is only in my dreams,

That I am not alone.

Diamond

by Any Pascual

The truth of life, Tail, is that a lot of people are going to use you. They only want you for the sake of interest, and if you want to survive, you're going to have to get used to it. If you don't understand that and don't know how to see what they intend, they can manipulate you. Take advantage of it, if you can, because there's a lot more to it than that. Hmm… Let me put it another way.

You see these walls, this mine we all grew up in? It's not just the rocks that are coal, we are coal, too. If someone thinks they are going to benefit from us, they grab their tools and chop us up, hurt us, crack us, tear us apart. Then they use our leftover pieces to warm themselves on cold nights. What they don't know is we have tools too, and we can chop, shape, break, and use to our own advantage.

Many relationships are like that, we are the coals of someone who uses us.

That's how the world works.

But, as with coal, sometimes there can be something else underneath it all. When coal endures adverse conditions, it transforms. It changes. It gets better.

Sometimes, underneath all that coal that ceases to be useful as soon as it's consumed in flames, there's something that doesn't give way. Something that remains, something that shines and glows thanks to the flames instead of being consumed.

That something is strong, and can bend others without breaking, but it doesn't need to, because it is stronger than everything else around it. That something is powerful, and therefore highly desired and tremendously protected. But it doesn't need that protection, because it is pure, and no matter how much circumstances shape it, it will never cease to be the way it is. Sometimes it hides in the most unsuspected places. Sometimes it masks and covers itself with several dark layers to blend in with its fellow coals. But in the end, it always shows its strength.

Do you know why? Because it does not bend before the picks and shovels of life.

Because, by stripping away those surface layers, those who seek to use are doing it a favor. They are letting its true self receive light. They are helping it be honest, with itself and with others.

Occasionally, it has to break the tools for that to happen, but usually its beauty speaks for itself and everyone in the mine recognizes that they have found something valuable. And it thanks the picks and shovels for helping it to be who it is and for helping them to understand, because it knows that without those challenges, without those obstacles, even without those problems, without those relationships, reasons, or circumstances, no one, not even that something, would have discovered its true value.

And then, over the years, that something can be polished and honed to the standards of picks and shovels. It may even be adored and valued. Perhaps it may even be a jewel, recognized and respected, displayed in many ways, always brightening and beautifying its surroundings.

But the most important thing is that it never loses perspective. It remembers the picks and shovels that can no longer hurt it. It remembers when it was smaller and less successful than it is now. It remembers when it couldn't even think that it would shine amongst all those black layers, when nature had not yet given it the endurance it now enjoys. It remembers everything, and it is grateful for it all. It wouldn't change a thing about those experiences, even if it could, because thanks to all it has been through, it has formed its great beauty and courage that is fostered more in self-love than in what others think. That strength that is already undeniable and inherent, that resilience that is so much its own. That spark that no one will ever take away, because you are who you are.

Those, Tail, are the people who are worth it and for whom we are alive: the diamond people.

And you know the best thing about all this? Every lump of coal has that possibility. Any person can be a diamond. We all have that spirit inside, deep down inside.

But, just like coal, most of us need to be spurred on by the harshest of our circumstances to know that we are diamonds, and a little humility to be kind to everyone. And all of us, even those who have been diamonds since the beginning of time, need impetus to share our true selves with others.

After all, that's what our picks and shovels were invented for. Don't you think?

Light at the End of the Tunnel

by Cheshta Sharma

His pen clicking in his fingers, Marco was lost to the world. The one in his head, that is. Lost enough to not catch the teacher calling his name a couple times, volume rising with each call.

"Marco."

His mind didn't register his name being called, too lost in his memories.

"*Marco.*"

The way she pushed her body in front of his, taking on the gunshots heading his way.

"Marco! Stop clicking your pen!"

The way that good-for-nothing street thug had turned and hightailed it as soon as he saw her figure drop to the ground, life draining from her body as the blood flowed out—

"Marco!"

The last one was loud enough to jar him out of his world. He flinched, the pen falling from his hand onto the desk with a clatter as his eyes shot up to the teacher now poised in front of his desk.

Before he could even think of anything to say, she beat him to it, her voice sharp as it rang through the room full of staring eyes. "Detention after school for not paying attention and disrupting class."

As his teacher turned back around and stalked to her place at the front of the classroom with her heels clacking irritatingly, she continued lecturing about how Richard Henry Lee had introduced a motion in Congress to declare independence in 1776.

Marco let his head drop and groaned quietly. *Amazing.*

† ┼ ┝

Walking into the library, Marco sighed quietly as he saw another student sorting the books, most likely having gotten detention like himself—he couldn't imagine anyone would do this for fun. He put his bag down on one of the tables, taking out his ear pods and starting his playlist, sighing in satisfaction as he heard *Solas* by Gibran Alcocer humming into ears, quieting his mind. He pocketed his phone, picking up the books scattered on the table and headed off to place them on their rightful shelves.

Just as he thought he could get some peace being in the company of books and music, a boy came up on his right, trying to engage in conversation. Marco recognized him as one of his classmates. Was his name Ash? Adrian? No. A-something. His name was A-something for now.

It seemed like A-something was quite the persistent guy. Marco successfully ignored two of his attempts before finally budging on the third.

"Hey uh—" Marco started.

"Hi!" A-something said enthusiastically.

Marco blinked in slight surprise and tried to match his energy in vain as he attempted to continue the conversation that had unexpectedly sparked. "Hey there, I, uh- I didn't see you, sorry."

"Oh, that's fine. I saw you here and we were the only ones with detention today—surprisingly—so decided to introduce myself. It makes sense though, us being the only ones here. It's a Monday and a lot of students are usually absent on Mondays. Anyways, I'm Leo. Leo Ferraro. What's your name?"

Never mind, his name *was not* A-something. Noted.

Clearing his throat, he replied. "I'm Marco. Just Marco."

"Well, Just Marco, what'd you do? To end up here I mean."

A huff escaped Marcos' lips. Maybe it was just his mood that was a bit down, but Leo was a tad too energetic—especially for a Monday. Who had the energy to be excited about anything on a *Monday*? Then again, Marco had the same level of enthusiasm every day of the week, so was he to judge. Plus, it seemed Leo was doing well with his fully functioning ability to be happy, so Marcus chided himself for being irritated.

It's not his fault you're stuck in the past, he told himself.

"Class disruption." He couldn't help the slight undertone of bitterness. "What about you?"

"Spoke up to Mr. Weyman about something he shouldn't have said."

A confused look flashed across Marco's face as Leo continued. Or tried to, at the very least. "He was—"

"Hey yoo thoo! Get back to werk! No cheet-chathing!" an accent Marco couldn't place his finger yelled at them from behind the librarian's desk.

Every kid in school knew the unspoken rule: don't mess with the librarian. One warning from the librarian was enough for Marco and Leo as they hastily went back to their tasks.

†✝†

Marco didn't know why he was surprised, but he found himself in the school bathroom having yet another panic attack. He'd been making his way out of school, practically feeling his social battery in the negatives when he thought to himself, *Okay. Just get out of school and get home and then you're safe. Then you'll be okay. You're almost out. Almost there. You're* so close.

Maybe it was the 'so close' that had triggered it. It was the last thing she'd said to him, so it made sense.

He gasped for air, but his throat felt like it was the thinnest pipe to ever exist because he just couldn't suck in a breath. And the panic that created in his mind—his very cells—was enough to make a fresh batch of tears roll down his face, which only led to more self-loathing. And didn't stop the wave of memories from rolling over him.

"Come on, Marco, we're almost there. We're—" A gasp. "—so close!" More gasping. Thundering footsteps, shouting and breathless gasps were all he could hear, along with the oddly loud heart beating in his chest. His adrenaline was so high he briefly wondered how he hadn't passed out yet. It was probably the fear.

A small part of him was grateful he wasn't alone in this situation they had found themselves in tonight. He had his aunt, his favorite person and role model, beside him. However much it soothed his anxiety though, it worsened it too. What if something happened—

"STOP!" A gunshot sounded. "Turn around!"

Marco fisted his hands in his hair, tugging at it, hoping, praying that the physical pain would be enough to distract him from his mental pain. It didn't work.

"Shut up! I- I'll shoot you. I'm not kidding. Don't-don't mess with me. I- I have a gun!" the thug stuttered out.

"Kid, this isn't the right way, please put the—" She had her hands out in a pacifying gesture, trying to calm the obviously amateur goon in front of them.

It was so like her—trying to help people no matter what, no matter how dangerous, how risky.

Before she could complete her sentence, it happened.

Just as Marco felt himself drowning in the murky depths of memories, he was yanked back to the surface, up and away from the terrifying waters. His hearing came back first.

"Marco!"

Then his sense of smell. Cinnamon. Marco liked cinnamon.

Then touch. The cold hard tiles, his body trembling, his cheeks cold and wet with tears, nose all snotty, chest aching and hands on both his shoulders.

Wait. Hands on his shoulders?

His vision was last. His head shot up to find Leo's face in front of his, concern written all over it like white paint on a black canvas.

"Hey… just breathe, alright? Focus on breathing. Breathe with me, slow and deep." Leo took one hand off his shoulders and gestured inhaling and exhaling.

Marco followed his instructions, too drained to resist and too scared to not accept help. Gradually, they got there.

Leo sat across a now calm Marco on the floor of the bathroom. Ideal first day with a guy you just met.

"I don't mean to sound intrusive, and you can totally not answer my question but— was it because of that incident with your aunt?"

Marco couldn't find it in himself to get mad. Sure, Leo was a bit tactless, but he truly cared. He cared enough to walk up to the quiet kid who didn't talk to anyone. He cared enough to actually try to talk to him— even though Marco had initially ignored him. He cared enough to help him out of a panic attack instead of just ignoring him and going home. He cared.

And even though he hated to admit it, Marco was in desperate   need   of   someone   who   cared. "Yeah."

Leo knew the answer already, of course. But he, quite evidently from his widened eyes, hadn't expected to be met with an actual answer.

Marco raised an eyebrow.

"How about we sit together at lunch tomorrow?"

Marco didn't know if he would ever move on, his aunt had practically raised him. But he'd realized after a month of his aunt being gone, that the loss of one relationship didn't stop him from being able to make new ones. Sure, he was terrified of losing another person, but then again, if you're scared to lose someone, it's only because you love them. He was willing to take that risk again because, God, did he miss loving others.

So here he was, befriending a guy his age. He dared to call it a step towards healing.

Marco had thought people lied about that 'light at the end of the tunnel' thing. Turns out they didn't.

Anisha Singh

Anisha Singh is a passionate author Mind lifelong learner. She is the author of *Soulful Reflections,* a poetry book that explores pain, love, and personal growth, and *Guardians of Green,* a children's ebook that teaches kids about caring for the environment.

Edited by Haley Kilgour

Anisha shares her insights on Medium under the username *@anishamwrites*, where she focuses on life lessons and personal stories that inspire others. Drawing inspiration from her love of sunsets and moongazing, she often reflects on how nature can heal and connect individuals to something greater. She believes that storytelling fosters unity in diversity, helping people find common ground and understanding. Through her commitment to mental health awareness, she aims to create a more compassionate world, inviting others to reflect on their lives and the larger narrative that binds us together.

Joyce Bou Charaa

Joyce Bou Charaa is a Lebanese writer and book editor. In 2020, during the lockdowns in Lebanon, Joyce started writing her first article on Agatha Christie's five best books and was published in *The Mark Literary Review*. From that moment, Joyce found a real passion in writing. She decided to expand her career as a writer of culture and literature, and later as a book editor.

Her articles have been published in *Aniko Press*, *Tint Journal*, *The Mark Literary Review*, *Newpages*, *Journal of Expressive Writing*, and *The Independent*. She has a BA in English from the Lebanese University.

Diya Lekshmi P. N.

Diya Lekshmi P.N is a 17-year-old writer from Kerala, India, who began her writing journey at a young age. With a passion for storytelling, she has explored various forms of creative writing, from short stories to poetry. Her work reflects a unique perspective shaped by her cultural background, life experiences her love for fantasy and human emotions.

Diya is an avid reader with a bias for fantasy and dystopian stories. She can be found on Instagram under @theheart_thecrown_thetear where she shares her love for books, photography, and her cats. She is also the

founder of Chronovue
(https://chronovue.wordpress.com/), a student journalism organization that provides opportunities for students around the world to express their passion for journalism.

Meredith Lindsey

Meredith Lindsey grew up in a patch of woods in southern Illinois that became inspiration for many stories. Currently employed as a Medical Laboratory Scientist, she keeps her fantasies alive by reading and writing about magic, paranormal beings, and anything more interesting than the mundane world. She currently lives in southern Indiana with her husband and German Shepherd.

Meredith's debut novel, *Letters in the Attic*, was awarded a bronze medal in the Readers' Favorite Book

Awards. Visit meredithlindsey.com to stay up to date on new book releases, exclusive content, and more!

Edited by Haley Kilgour

H. C. Kilgour

Growing up, you were just as likely to find H. C. playing outside as you were to find her with her nose in a book. She particularly enjoys books focusing on worlds of magic and adventure.

Often joking that she's part mermaid, H. C. pursued a marine biology degree from the University of North

Carolina Wilmington, graduating in 2017. She then proceeded to attend the University of Miami earing a Master of Professional Science in marine conservation in 2019.

She says her biggest inspiration for writing is that she simply needs her characters to be quiet, so she can think. H. C. had a colorful upbringing in Charlotte, North Carolina, which she has accentuated by traveling as much as she can. She currently lives in Key Largo with her husband and two cats.

H. C. is co-owner of Owl Talyn Press, started with David F. Balog in 2023. Through Owl Talyn Press, H. C. hopes readers and authors can find their OPT or One True Pairing. Her first two novels, Nanagin and Ravliean, are just that, the beginning. Follower H. C. on Instagram under @by_hckilgour!

Laura Lukasavage

Laura Lukasavage started writing shortly after her mother's passing when she was only fourteen years old. She remembered how her mom would write poems and letters to her stepdad, and, as a way to feel close to her mother, she took up writing. She started with poems in eighth grade and then short stories in high school. Once she started college in 2009 at Neumann University, her interest only grew. By the time she transfered from Neumann University to Rowan University in 2011 after her father's passing, she knew what her passions truly were.

She majored in Radio, TV, and Film productions with a minor in creative writing. She found her love of film and writing meshed well, and this is where she felt at peace. Laura writes as a way to escape from reality but also to deal with life as a whole. She writes hoping that one day her books will be an escape for someone needing them.

Edited by Haley Kilgour

David F. Balog

David F. Balog was born, raised, and still lives in the greater Cleveland area. Ever inquisitive, he dove deeply into science, paranormal studies, mathematics, and mythology at an early age, and never let go of the idea that they were all tightly connected.

An avid reader, particularly, but certainly not limited to, science and science fiction, David always sought to learn more about the world. His personal studies eventually clashed with his scholastic teachings, causing him to reject traditional academia for a time. Years later, he would earn a Master's Degree in History. Through his studies, he continued to focus on theology, mythology, and fables and how they connected societies throughout time and regions.

His fascination with fables and mythology led him first to Dungeons & Dragons, then other role-playing games. Here, he learned to hone his talent for character creation, world building, and storytelling. Over time, basic concepts became fully realized, and months and years spent focused on a single character gave time for them to develop depth.

At long last, it fell on David to contribute his own stories and mythologies to the public. With the experience of developing characters and worlds combined with writing numerous research papers, David began work on his first novel: *Necromancer's Lament*, the first in a planned trilogy, soon followed by *Necromancer's Sorrow*.

In 2023, David started Owl Talyn Press with H. C. Kilgour. Together they strive to create a home for authors and their works. And, of course, they also strive to share their love of fantasy. Catch David as the Cleveland local Odd Mall events and follow him on Instagram at @david.f.balog.

Any Pascual

Any Pascual, born in 2004, is a Spanish poet, blogger, speaker, and Highly Sensitive Person. She is a Christian creative, a soul whose purpose is to love, understand, and convey love. *Diamond* is her first short story in English, a tale about resilience and realizing our inner strength. If you find yourself reflected in what it says, if you are moved by her words, then this story has fulfilled its purpose.

Any is the self-published author of various cozy poetry books for sensitive souls, including *Sensitivity: Poems of a Highly Sensitive Teenager, A year in verses: Poem diary,* and her upcoming collection *Caves and Forests: Natural poetry.*

She has been writing and sharing her work for many years on various platforms. You can find her at anayany.com, @any_espiritual on Instagram, X and TikTok, and @anyespiritual on Facebook.

She enjoys supporting other authors, connecting with fellow readers, and having meaningful conversations with her friends. So please, reach out and say hi!

Cheshta Sharma

Cheshta Sharma is a talented teen author and aspiring poet whose words weave vivid tales and heartfelt verses.

Shadows of the Mind

A curious soul and voracious reader, she is often found immersed in the pages of a book. A naturalist at heart and an avid shutterbug, Cheshta draws inspiration from the beauty of the skies, the serenity of nighttime, and the wonders of nature. With a fiery passion for debates and a flair for creative writing, her boundless imagination brings her stories and poems to life.
Cheshta is the author of *Exorcise My Heart*, a gripping horror-thriller novelette.

Her forthcoming poetry collection, *Thoughts of a Midnight Whisperer*, promises an evocative journey through love, grief, madness, and healing, showcasing her poetic mastery.

You can connect with Cheshta and explore her literary musings on Instagram at @cogitationes_nocte.

Letter from the Editor

Hi everyone!

Wow, thank you for making it all the way to the end of this anthology. I know when I speak, I speak not only for myself, but for all the authors represented in this anthology. Thank you for reading. Thank you for supporting us and in turn the charity this book supports.

This anthology started as an idea in an author chat in the summer of 2024. Not going to lie, it was like herding cats for a little while. As a group, we had some kinks to work out. But, clearly, we figured it out.

A lot of us, if not all of us, have imperfect mental health. As authors, we wanted to take a topic close to our hearts and find a way to speak up, heal, and support others. As the editor, I think all the authors nailed it. Each piece speaks from the heart and soul.

Obviously, this book wouldn't be possible without the many authors that contributed to this book. But a special thank you is due to Any Pascual who spearheaded this whole thing by suggesting we write an anthology.

We also need to thank Owl Talyn Press for welcoming this anthology into their nest with open arms. Without the Owl Talyn Press staff, this book would just be stories floating in the ether.

To all those reading this book, we hope you can find yourself in our stories. And that our stories can help you down a path of healing. Or maybe they help you understand a loved one just a little better. Either way, we hope these stories stay with you.

With much love,
H. C. Kilgour

www.ingramcontent.com/pod-product-compliance
Lightning Source LLC
Chambersburg PA
CBHW071132100726
47908CB00008B/2575